THE KITCHEN KNIGHT

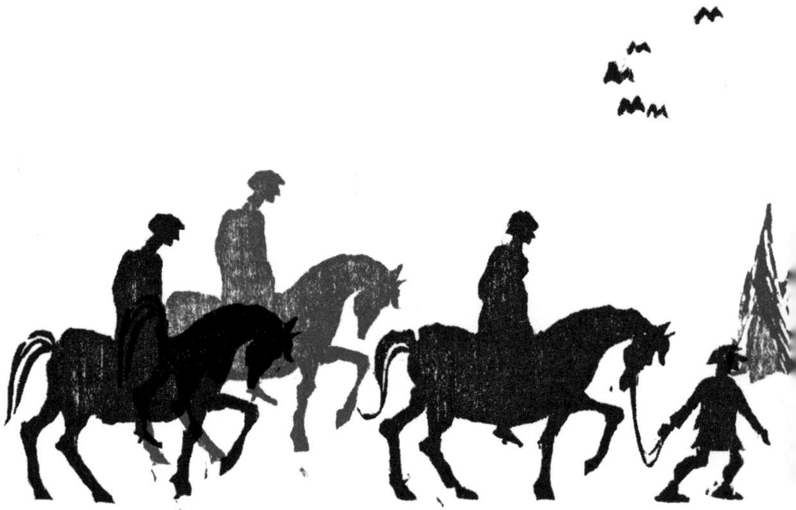

The Kitchen Knight

ADAPTED AND RETOLD BY BARBARA SCHILLER

ILLUSTRATED BY NONNY HOGROGIAN

HOLT, RINEHART AND WINSTON

NEW YORK · CHICAGO · SAN FRANCISCO

FOR THOMAS

This adaptation is based on *The Works of Sir Thomas Malory*, edited by Eugène Vinaver, Oxford University Press, and Malory's *Le Morte D'Arthur*, a new rendition by Keith Baines, Clarkson N. Potter, Inc.

AUTHOR'S NOTE

A consistent excuse in adapting from authors of long ago is that they in turn had borrowed from earlier writers. This is quite true. Sir Thomas Malory borrowed from one English poem and three lengthy French books of the thirteenth century.

He modernized his sources by reducing their oratorical qualities and simplifying and strengthening the ornate style and story lines. *The Tale of Sir Gareth of Orkeney That Was Called Bewmaynes* is considered one of the best examples, in Eugène Vinaver's words, "of the technique of a modern tale applied to medieval romance." Further, it exemplifies in a straightforward and colorful fashion Malory's ideas of chivalry. And it is a good story of adventure and romance.

So when I was thinking of a way to introduce young children to the delights of Arthurian legend, the story of Gareth seemed perfect. I have condensed the plot a bit and simplified the ending without, I hope, sacrificing the spirit, tone, and intent of the original.

BARBARA SCHILLER

THE KNIGHTS OF THE ROUND TABLE had gathered at Pentecost time in a castle upon the coast of Wales. There they renewed their knightly vows to aid all gentlewomen, to be merciful, just, and true.

Now in this season King Arthur had the special custom of not sitting down to celebrate the feast of Pentecost until he had heard or seen a great marvel.

A little before noon of this day, Sir Gawain, the King's nephew, saw from a window three men on horseback accompanied by a dwarf. The three men dismounted and, leaving their horses with the dwarf, approached the castle gate.

Then Sir Gawain went into the great hall and said to the King, "Sire, let us sit down to our feast, for here come three men who will surely bring strange tidings."

As he finished, the three men entered the hall. Two were gentlemen richly clad and between them walked a tall young man, fair of face, with hands that were large and beautiful.

The youth stood tall before King Arthur.

"Noble King, may God bless you and your Knights of the Round Table. I have come to ask of you three simple gifts. One I shall ask now, the other two at the next feast of the Pentecost."

"Ask," said the King, "and the gifts shall be yours."

"Sire, I request of you to give me food and lodging for a year. In twelve month's time I will come before you again to ask my remaining two gifts."

There was a murmur of surprise throughout the great hall.

"Fair youth," said the King. "This I would grant to any man. Ask of me a gift more in keeping with your noble manner."

"At this time I will ask nothing else."

"So be it. But tell me your name."

When the young man politely refused, the King and his knights found this very odd.

Turning then to Sir Kay, the Steward, King Arthur ordered him to treat the youth as befits one of noble blood.

"Ha!" sneered Sir Kay. "That would be a waste. For surely this fellow comes from hut or stable. If he were of gentle birth he would have asked for horse, sword, and armor. But I will keep him in the kitchen and stuff him full of good food till he is fat as a pig."

Looking scornfully at the lad, Sir Kay went on, "And since he has no name, I shall give him one—Fairhands."

The youth bowed his head and his two companions left the hall and rode away.

9

Fairhands went into the kitchen that was to be his home for the next twelve months. It was a vast, vaulted chamber with four open hearths, one smoke hole, and a multitude of men and boys dashing to and fro.

Daily Fairhands stoked the fires, turned the spit, and scrubbed the pots. At night he lay down with the other kitchen boys upon a heap of straw. And month after month he bore with patience Sir Kay's sharp and spiteful tongue.

Sir Lancelot, out of the goodness of his heart and for shame of Sir Kay's manner, offered Fairhands clothes and money for his needs. And Sir Gawain did likewise, but less from courtesy than from an unexplainable sense of kinship with the youth.

But Fairhands refused them both, and stayed in the kitchen, forever at Sir Kay's beck and call.

However, if there was a display of knightly skills at tournament or joust, then Fairhands would hurry from the kitchen to watch.

And whenever the servant boys played at running, jumping, and throwing, Sir Kay should have been proud of his kitchen boy, for Fairhands was always first.

So the days passed and springtime came again, bringing with it the feast of Pentecost. Once again Arthur and his knights waited to hear of an unusual adventure before sitting down at the Round Table.

Then a squire ran into the hall and said to the King, "Sire, you may go to your feast, for a lady has come with some strange tale to relate."

When Arthur and his knights were seated, a young lady entered the hall and knelt before the King's throne.

12

"Sir King, my sister, a lady of high degree and broad domains, has been besieged for two years in her castle by a tyrannical knight. I beg of you to send one of your knights to her rescue."

"Fair lady, tell me your sister's name, and where she lives, and who the man is who holds her captive," Arthur responded.

"The first two questions I may not answer. But as to her besieger, he is called the Red Knight of the Red Lands."

Sir Gawain rose from his chair. "I know him well! I fought with him once and barely escaped with my life."

"Nevertheless," said Arthur, "I cannot send one of my knights on this quest unless I know your sister's name and where she dwells."

The lady turned away from the King. "Then I must look elsewhere for aid!"

"Wait!" cried a voice from the back of the hall.

Fairhands stepped forward. "Noble King, for twelve months I have lived in your kitchen. Now the time has come for me to ask of you the two other gifts."

"Ask then, Fairhands."

"The first is that you allow me to aid this lady. The second is that you permit Sir Lancelot to ride after me. When I have proved myself worthy, I wish to be knighted by the hand of he who is the truest of men and the bravest of knights."

"All of this shall be done," said the King.

The lady turned on Arthur. "You do wrong to shame me this way. How dare you send a kitchen boy to be my sister's champion!" With that she marched angrily from the hall.

Meanwhile, Fairhands' dwarf had come again, leading a splendid white war horse bedecked with cloth-of-gold trappings and carrying armor and sword of the richest workmanship.

14

All the knights wondered at Fairhands' fine equipment and noble appearance as he rode out through the castle gate.

But Sir Kay was angry. Fully armed and mounted, he announced to the court that he would show the kitchen boy who his master was.

Riding hard, he caught up with Fairhands. 16

"Ho, boy! Do you know me for your better?"

"Sir Kay, I know you only as the most ungracious knight at Arthur's court. Now fight, if you will!"

The Steward lowered his spear and charged. Fairhands, who had neither spear nor shield, met him squarely and with the first stroke of his sword knocked the spear from Sir Kay's mailed fist. The second stroke dashed the proud steward to the ground where he lay as if dead.

"Now," laughed Fairhands, picking up Sir Kay's spear and shield, "I lack nothing in the way of knightly weapons."

Just then Sir Lancelot, who had witnessed the encounter from afar, rode up.

Fairhands gave Sir Kay's horse to his dwarf and remounted his own charger.

"Gentle knight," he called to Lancelot. "Will you joust?"

17

For answer, Lancelot lowered his visor and couched his spear.

They galloped at each other with such force that both were thrown to the ground. Throwing aside their shields they fought on foot with the ferocity of wild boars.

Sir Lancelot, marveling at the young man's great strength, stepped back. "Hold, Fairhands. We have no reason to quarrel."

The youth lowered his sword. "You speak the truth. Still it feels good to fight hard and not tire."

Lancelot laughed a little grimly. "Speak for yourself. I was beginning to fear that I would have to sue for mercy."

"If that is so, then am I worthy to be made a knight?"

"Certainly, but first you must tell me who you truly are."

"If you will not reveal my secret."

"On my faith, Fairhands, I shall not." 18

"My name is Gareth of Orkney. I am the younger brother by many years of Sir Gawain."

Lancelot clasped the youth's hand. "You make me glad, for I guessed that you were more than a seeker of meat and drink."

The older knight then bestowed on him the order of knighthood, and galloped away to carry Sir Kay back to the castle.

Fairhands turned his horse and rode through the forest after the lady. None of the spring birds that sang sweetly among the tender green leaves could match in happiness the joy in the young knight's heart as he set forth on his first great adventure.

But no sooner did he overtake the lady than she rounded on him.

"Why do you follow me, you dirty kitchen knave? Get back to your pots and pans. Hurry!"

"Lady," sighed Fairhands, "say what you will, but I have undertaken this quest and nothing shall stop me."

The lady sniffed. "Greasy ladle washer, you'll turn tail fast enough when we meet real danger."

Soon they came to a fast-flowing river. On the bank opposite waited two grim knights, their spears poised for combat.

"Scurry back to the kitchen, scullion, and save your skin while you can," warned the lady.

"No. Were there six more knights I would not flee."

With that, Fairhands urged his horse into the river. The first of the knights galloped to meet him in the middle of the stream, where they broke their spears on each other's armor. At once, they drew their swords and went at each other eagerly. Fairhands smote his opponent a stunning blow on the helmet and knocked him into the water.

The second knight, seeing his companion drowned, waited on the bank for Fairhands to come closer.

They clashed together with a roar like thunder, and the knight's spear splintered. With a mighty stroke Fairhands dealt him a death blow across the visor.

He then joined the lady and suggested they continue on their way.

"It is most strange," said she, "that fortune should favor a kitchen knight like you. Be assured that it was not your strength or courage that overcame those two brave knights. The first was drowned in the water when his horse stumbled. And the second, poor man, was laid low by a cowardly blow from behind. Why don't you turn back while you can? I say this for your own good, for surely the next knight we meet will despatch you from this life in short order."

"Lady," replied Fairhands, spurring his horse, "I have sworn to help your sister. Let us ride on."

The sun was slanting low through the trees when they came to a woodsman's hut.

There they had a simple meal of bread and cheese, accompanied all the while by the lady's scornful talk and haughty ways.

Night brought respite, but in the early morning hours as they continued on their journey, Fairhands knew little peace from his cruel-tongued companion.

23

Now they were deep within the great forest. The trees grew closer together and their leafy branches hid all but a glimmer of daylight.

It was afternoon when Sir Fairhands and the lady came to a shadowed glade. There on a black hawthorn hung a black shield and banner. Nearby waited a knight in black armor upon a black horse, a long spear in his right hand.

"Well, my lady," said he, "is this the knight you brought from King Arthur's court to be your champion?"

"No, brave knight. This is but a kitchen lackey aping his betters. He is a greasy beggar who follows me against my will."

"I shall put a stop to that! It is not honorable for me to fight such as he, but I'll strip him of horse and armor and let him feel the flat of my sword on his back. Be assured that he will run yelping home to his pots and pans."

"Black Knight, you seem very eager to have my horse and armor. Fight for them then!"

"With a kitchen knave! What do you take me for?"

"For a man of less noble birth than mine," roared Fairhands. "And I shall prove it!"

Angered beyond reason, both knights charged at a headlong gallop. Their spears broken, they rushed at each other with drawn swords. Although the point of Fairhands' spear was embedded in his side, the Black Knight gave the youth many a cruel blow. But at last, after fighting for an hour and a half, he fell from his horse and died.

The lady spurred her horse and Fairhands rode after her.

"Alas," she said when he came near, "that an oafish kitchen knight should have the luck to slay such a noble man. But I warn you that good fortune will desert you. Close by is a knight who will demand full payment for the wrongs you have done. Turn back while there is still time."

"Lady, it is of no use to scold and scoff. I will see this journey to the end come what may."

They had traveled scarcely more than a mile when a knight armored all in green crossed their path at a slow canter.

Upon seeing the lady and Fairhands he checked his horse and turned towards them.

"Greetings to you, my lady, and to you, Sir Knight."

"You would not say that, Green Knight," she replied, "if you knew who this knave is and what he has done."

The knight pushed up his visor and looked at Fairhands. "I would judge him to be a gentle knight with brave deeds to his credit."

"Sir, you are deceived. This is the lowly ladle washer from King Arthur's kitchen who has killed your brother the Black Knight by trick and by treachery."

"Villain!" cried the Green Knight. "You shall die for the murder of my brother."

"I defy you!" said Fairhands. "I killed him honorably in knightly combat."

For an answer, the Green Knight blew three shrill notes on his hunting horn. As the last note died away, two maidens appeared. One handed her master a green shield, the other a green spear.

The two men drew apart and then came at each other like champions. Their spears splintered down to their fists.

Drawing swords they slashed and thrust at each other until Fairhands by an overstroke wounded his opponent's charger. As the horse fell, the Green Knight jumped clear and prepared to fight on foot. Fairhands leaped from the saddle and they clashed at close quarters. Breathless and bleeding, neither knight would yield, and thus they fought for a long while.

At last the lady spoke up. "For shame that a true knight should let a kitchen knave prove his match."

Ashamed, the Green Knight summoned his strength and hewed his opponent's shield in half.

With that, Fairhands whirled his sword over his head and brought it down in a mighty buffet upon the Green Knight's helmet.

Driven to his knees, the knight cried for mercy.

"You ask in vain," answered Fairhands, "unless the lady will plead for your life."

"I would never ask a favor from such as you!" she said.

Fairhands drew his dagger.

"Wait," begged the Green Knight. "Do not let me die for want of a lady's word. I shall forgive you my brother's death and swear allegiance to you if I am spared."

Fairhands looked to the lady who angrily turned her head aside.

"So be it," said Fairhands, placing his dagger to the Green Knight's throat.

"Stop, knave—or you will repent your deed."

Bowing to the lady, Fairhands replied. "Your word is my command, for in nothing would I cause you displeasure."

Ignoring him, the lady turned to the Green Knight with a sweet smile. "My lord, I must ask of you a favor. Would you ride with me through the forest, for I find it a most dark and dangerous place."

"Lady, it seems to me that this brave knight offers you all the protection that could be desired. Nevertheless, I will guide you both through the forest in the morning. Tonight you shall be guests at my castle."

The two knights rode through the woodland paths with the lady in scornful silence between them and the dwarf behind.

The Green Knight's castle lay in a large clearing in the forest. Fairhands noted the strength of the gatehouse towers and, as they

clattered into the court, the thick walls of the fine square keep.

Once in the hall, the Green Knight ordered a servant to show Fairhands to his chamber and tend his wounds.

Refreshed and relieved of his armor, the young knight then joined his host and the lady at the high table.

It would have been a merry meal if the lady had bridled her tongue. But above the sweet music of the minstrels, her voice sounded loud, clear, and scornful.

At last the Green Knight turned toward her.

"It astonishes me that such unseemly words should be directed to so worthy a gentleman as Sir Fairhands. Surely he has by now proved to you, as he has to me, the strength of his sword and the courage of his spirit. Further, I warn you, that whatever he pretends concerning his birth, he will one day be revealed as a man of the noblest blood."

The lady rose from her seat. "Your words cause me equal astonishment, my lord. And now excuse me, for I cannot bring myself to share a table with this smelly scullion a moment more."

In the morning after they had broken their fast with bread, ale, and beef, the Green Knight led his guests to the forest's edge. There he knelt and did Fairhands homage while the lady tapped her foot in anger and impatience.

Their journey took them now through a land of rolling hills and flowered fields. Except for the song of the birds and the sigh of the wind, they rode in silence.

As they came to the top of a hill somewhat higher than the rest, the lady held up her hand.

"Stop, knave, and look below you."

Fairhands reined in his horse and saw below him a green plain of new-mown grass jeweled with silken tents and pavilions. Beyond it stood a beautiful city of white spires and towers encircled by a high wall of gleaming stone.

"All this belongs to a lord of great glory and honor. A knight who commands five hundred men of high degree. A gentleman who passes the time of day in knightly joust and tournament.

"Look," she said as they continued down the hill, "there is his pavilion, topmost of them all and the color of indigo as are all things that belong to him."

"What is this valiant knight's name?"

"He is called Sir Persaunt, the Indigo Knight. You would do well to tremble and flee before he sees you, for it is his custom to challenge every knight who crosses his domain."

"Lady," replied Fairhands courteously but coldly, "before every combat you call me a coward, and afterward you deny to me what I have accomplished. Yet I will once again challenge any man who bars our way. If the Indigo

Knight is a man of great honor, then greater
will be my honor if I overcome him."

"Ah," said the lady. "I am beginning to
believe you are indeed a gentleman of high
chivalry, well worthy to rescue my sister. And
it is for this reason that I beg you not to accept
the Indigo Knight's challenge. You and your
horse have suffered much and I would not have
you wounded any more. My sister's castle is

only seven miles from here and you will need all your strength to combat the knight who holds her captive."

"I should be ashamed to come so near a knight and refuse him combat. Trust in God and we shall come safely through this passage."

The lady checked her horse and looked at Fairhands. "Now I know you are a man of noble birth."

She rode on a while. "Will you forgive me the rudeness I have shown you?"

Fairhands smiled. "Yes, my lady."

Then, putting spurs to his horse, he gaily cried, "Whereas anger at your cruel ways had made me strong, now good cheer at your kind words shall make me invincible!"

Soon they saw a messenger dressed in indigo silk riding toward them.

The messenger halted and spoke. "I come from Sir Persaunt, the Indigo Knight. He asks whether you come in war or in peace."

"Tell your master that I offer a challenge only if he wishes to receive one."

The messenger saluted and rode back across the field to his lord's pavilion.

Before long Fairhands saw the Indigo Knight, dressed for combat, galloping toward them.

The young knight made himself ready, and the two men clashed together with all their might. Such was the force of their encounter that their spears were shattered and their horses thrown to the ground.

Holding their shields before them, the two knights drew their swords and advanced on foot towards each other.

For two hours they fought, each giving and receiving sword strokes so mighty that their armor and shields were battered and broken. At last, Fairhands was able to wound his opponent deeply, but still the Indigo Knight fought bravely on.

37

Finally, although he was reluctant to do so, Fairhands brought his sword with stunning force down upon Sir Persaunt's helmet.

As the Indigo Knight lay stretched out on the field, Fairhands kneeled down and drew his dagger.

Seeing the weapon pointed at his throat, Sir Persaunt yielded at once.

"Sir Fairhands," begged the lady, "spare the life of this brave gentleman."

Fairhands rose and helped Sir Persaunt to his feet. "Gladly, for it would be a pity for such a noble knight to die."

"Many thanks," replied the Indigo Knight. "Now I know indeed that you are the man who killed my brother the Black Knight and won over my second brother the Green Knight. And as he swore allegiance to you, so shall I."

Sir Persaunt then led Fairhands and the lady to his pavilion where they rested and refreshed themselves with wine and spices.

38

Later that evening they rode into the city with the Indigo Knight and his company to dine in the castle.

The next morning as they were taking their leave, Sir Persaunt asked the lady where she was leading Sir Fairhands.

"To the Castle Dangerous where my sister is besieged."

"Aha! that is the work of the Red Knight of the Red Lands. And the castle belongs to the Lady Lyoness whom men say is the fairest lady in the kingdom. Then surely you are the Lady Lynet?"

"That is my name."

The Indigo Knight now turned to Fairhands. "I must warn you of this Red Knight. He is the most dangerous knight in the land, a man completely without mercy, a champion whose strength is equal to that of seven men. But your cause is as worthy as it is perilous. Lady Lyoness has been held captive in her own castle for two years while the Red Knight has used her lands as if they were his own."

"I pray," said Fairhands, "that soon she shall be at his mercy no longer. But why does this cruel knight tarry so long at the siege?"

"Because he is waiting to be challenged by one of the four knights of the Round Table whom he considers to be the most powerful. So until Sir Lancelot, Sir Tristram, Sir Gawain, or Sir Lamerok offer him battle, the Red Knight will hold the Lady Lyoness a prisoner."

The Indigo Knight held out his hand to his guest. "Godspeed, Sir Fairhands. Be strong and of good heart."

"Sir Persaunt, I thank you for your goodwill. And now if you and Lady Lynet will swear to keep my secret, I shall tell you my true identity."

"We swear," said the knight and the lady together.

"My name is Gareth of Orkney. King Lot was my father. My mother is King Arthur's sister. My brother is Sir Gawain. Except for Sir Lancelot, no one at Arthur's court knows who I am."

Now while his master was talking with the Indigo Knight, the dwarf slipped away and rode as fast as he could to the Castle Dangerous.

Hiding in a wagon laden with firewood, he entered the castle and then made his way to the Lady Lyoness' bower.

His sudden entrance caused her surprise but not fright. The dwarf was pleased that his master's lady was not only of surpassing beauty but of brave heart as well.

Quickly he told her that Lynet was bringing a knight of King Arthur's court to be her champion.

There was little hope in her soft voice as she asked what manner of man this knight was.

"A noble warrior and as fair a man as you are a lady. Although young, he is worthy enough to have been knighted by the great Lancelot. And brave enough to have come through the Passage Perilous," added the dwarf.

Lyoness' fair face brightened. "How did your master escape from the powerful knights who challenge all who dare this passage?"

"First he killed the two brothers who waited at the river."

"Good riddance," said Lyoness. "They were little better than murderers."

The dwarf nodded and continued. "Then my master killed the Black Knight. Next he fought the Green Knight and overcame him. Finally, he vanquished the Indigo Knight, at whose castle he is now."

The lady smiled and her beauty blazed forth like the morning sun. "Your master is truly brave and worthy. But you have not mentioned my champion's name and rank."

"I have sworn not to reveal that. I can tell you only that he wishes to be called by the name of Fairhands and that he is of the royal house of Orkney."

"Dwarf," said Lyoness, "your tidings have brought happiness back to my life. Now listen closely to what I wish you to do."

The dwarf came close to the lady's chair.

"Go to the hermitage nearby and deliver into the hands of the hermit wine, venison, and roasted chicken, all of the best quality and in good quantity."

Lyoness went to a cupboard and opened it.

"Take this also, my great cup of gold and precious jewels. Then ride with all speed to my sister and Sir Fairhands. Give them my good wishes and lead them to the hermitage. Tell your master to eat well and sleep soundly, for he will need all his strength and wits to deal with the Red Knight of the Red Lands. But tell him also to be of good cheer and stout heart, because my besieger is a cruel man to whom I could never yield."

The dwarf bowed low and departed. When he reached Sir Persaunt's castle he told the two knights and the lady about his meeting with Lyoness.

The Indigo Knight rode with them half the way to the hermitage and then, wishing Fairhands good fortune, turned his horse homeward.

Now it was but a short ride to the hermit's house. The dwarf knocked loudly on the door and the hermit hastened to make them welcome.

As soon as Fairhands and Lynet had eaten the meat and drunk the wine, the dwarf took the golden cup back to Lyoness.

As he was leaving Castle Dangerous the dwarf felt a heavy hand upon his shoulder. Turning around he found himself facing the Red Knight of the Red Lands.

"What tidings do you bring, Dwarf?"

"Sir, I have been with the Lady Lynet and the champion she has brought from King Arthur's court."

46

The Red Knight smiled grimly. "Unless she has with her Sir Lancelot, Sir Tristram, Sir Lamerok, or Sir Gawain, she has wasted her time and that of the knight."

"Think that if you will, but this champion has fought his way through the Passage Perilous."

"Oho! Then she has brought one of these four great knights?"

"No, but he is a man of royal birth whose name I cannot reveal."

The Red Knight yawned. "Then I am not interested in his name. I shall deal with him as I have done with those who came before him."

"And a most disgraceful way that is," said the dwarf as he scurried away from the castle.

On the next day after breakfast, Fairhands and Lynet rode from the hermitage. Their way took them through a fair forest and across a wide plain sweeping down to the sea.

This plain bristled with siege weapons and armed men, tents and pavilions. By the shore Castle Dangerous lifted its towers to the sky.

It was a fine sight for a warrior to see, and Fairhands felt the joy of battle in his heart. But then as they rode past a grove of trees his face turned pale. For on forty trees hung forty knights clothed in full armor, their swords at their sides.

"What is the meaning of this?" he gasped.

"These are the knights who have tried to rescue my sister. When the Red Knight overcomes a challenger, this is how he treats him."

"Preserve me from such a disgraceful death!" exclaimed Fairhands.

"Do not lose courage, I beg you. You will need a full measure to face the Red Knight."

They continued in silence up to the castle moats, formed by double dikes which were filled from the sea. A fleet of ships stood anchored in the water, and everywhere there

48

was ceaseless activity and the sound of music and merriment.

To one side of the castle gate grew a tall sycamore. Upon this the Red Knight had hung a huge ivory horn for those who dared to challenge him.

Fairhands spurred his horse, galloped to the sycamore, and blew the horn so eagerly that all the company of the siege and the castle stopped what they were doing. Then

49

knights and ladies, servants and soldiers rushed from all directions to watch the coming battle.

Within his pavilion the Red Knight waited impatiently while his lords and barons armed him, buckled his spurs, and handed him shield, sword, and spear. Then clad all in brilliant red, he rode to a small hollow in good view of both his company and the castle.

"Fairhands," said Lynet, "here comes your deadly enemy, and there at the tower window watches my sister."

"Where?" asked the young knight eagerly.

Lynet pointed to a window in the tower nearest them. Fairhands' heart leaped at the sight of the most beautiful lady he had ever looked upon.

Lyoness curtsied to her champion and then held out her hands in supplication.

Fairhands bowed low to her. "I know no better cause to do battle for than that of a lady whose beauty surpasses all."

"Cease looking at the Lady Lyoness," shouted the Red Knight, "and look to your weapons instead. She is *my* lady and many are the knights I have killed for her sake."

"Then you have murdered in vain. I know that she holds no love for you and that she is glad of my coming."

Looking up at Lyoness once again, Fairhands continued. "Now that I have seen my lady, I know that I love her and will rescue her, or die in the attempt."

"Sir Knight, in your last words you most surely spoke the truth. But enough of talk. Make ready to fight!"

Positioning their spears, they rode at each other with such force that both crashed to the ground. So violent was the impact that the onlookers judged both knights dead.

But the warriors regained consciousness and went at each other with hard chopping strokes to the body and head. First one would stagger and then the other, but neither fell under the steady hail of blows.

So they fought until well past noontime, when they paused to gain their breath.

Leaning upon their swords they rested a while before returning to battle. Their shields were chipped and cracked now and their armor was battered and broken in places.

The Red Knight was shrewd and Fairhands was hard put to defend those places where his armor no longer gave protection.

Still they came at each other with unmatched ferocity. When one or the other fell to the ground half stunned, his opponent would leap on top of him. More than once the knights exchanged swords by accident.

At eventide when Fairhands and the Red Knight agreed to rest, there was none among the onlookers who could predict the battle's outcome.

The dwarf unlaced his master's helmet

and drew it off so he could gain refreshment from the cooling sea breeze. The Red Knight's page did likewise, and so the two men sat near the field of combat.

Fairhands looked up at the tower window where Lyoness watched. So loving was her smile that not only did fatigue drop from him, but hope and courage returned with a joyful surge.

He jumped lightly to his feet and asked the Red Knight to prepare again for battle.

"Right willingly," replied the knight, "and to the death!"

Despite their wounds, they fought as men fresh to battle. Then the Red Knight dealt Fairhands two powerful and skillful blows. The first sent the young man's sword spinning from his hand, the second hurled him to the ground.

As Fairhands struggled to keep the Red Knight's dagger from his throat, he heard Lynet calling to him.

"Fairhands! Fairhands! My sister weeps at your plight. Gather your strength that you might stop her tears."

Hearing these words, Fairhands managed to thrust his opponent from him. Then, reaching desperately for his sword, he leaped to his feet and confronted the Red Knight once more.

But now Fairhands fought like a man possessed. He doubled his strokes until, at last, the Red Knight's sword went flying. Pressing the advantage, Fairhands rained blows upon his opponent's helmet. Then the Red Knight sank to the ground and the youth leaped on top of him, drawing his dagger.

"Fairhands, I beg you for mercy!" cried the Red Knight in a voice that all could hear.

Thinking of the forty knights in the grove of trees, Fairhands shook his head and proceeded to unlace the Red Knight's helmet.

"I cannot honorably spare a knight who treats his challengers as shamefully as you have done."

"Hold your hand, noble knight, and I shall tell you the reason."

"Speak on," said Fairhands.

"Once I loved a fair lady whose brothers had been killed by Sir Gawain and Sir Lancelot. As the lady's sworn champion I was bound to obey her in all things. So when she asked me to challenge every knight of King Arthur's court who chanced by, I could not refuse. And when further she demanded that I hang each vanquished knight until I met Sir Lancelot and Sir Gawain, I did so for the sake of the lady and my knightly oath."

As the Red Knight fell silent, his earls and barons gathered round and threw themselves to their knees.

They begged Fairhands to spare the Red Knight's life.

"Nothing will be gained by his death," they said. "His misdeeds cannot be undone however much he may wish it. But if you let him live, then he can pay homage to you and make amends for his ill-spent past."

"My lords," replied Fairhands, "since all that the Red Knight did was at the asking of a lady I blame him the less. For your sake I will release him if he swears to my conditions. First, he must yield himself to the Lady Lyoness, obtain her pardon, and make redress for all the wrongs he has done to her."

"Agreed," said the Red Knight.

"Then he must go to the court of King Arthur and confess his enmity towards Sir Gawain and Sir Lancelot."

"Gladly will I do what you ask of me," answered the Red Knight, rising to his feet.

Before entering the castle, he ordered his companions to lead Fairhands to his pavilion and treat the young knight as their lord and master.

The moon was well up in the sky when the Red Knight returned.

"Noble sir," he said to Fairhands, "the Lady Lyoness has forgiven me and accepted my oath to redress the wrongs I have done. Tomorrow morning I shall ride with my company to King Arthur's court to fulfill my second obligation. And now Lady Lyoness has requested that her sister come to the castle and there pass the night."

So saying, he bowed and departed with Lynet.

The next morning before breakfast the Red Knight and his men gathered before Fairhands' pavilion. When the young knight appeared, they kneeled and paid him homage.

Fairhands watched them depart and then returned to the pavilion. There he found Lynet.

"I come with a message from my sister. She wishes to see you."

Joyously Fairhands armed and mounted and galloped straight toward his lady's castle.

As he neared the gate his delight turned to dismay. The drawbridge was raised. The portcullis was down. And armed men stood on the gatehouse walls.

Lyoness watched from a window, her hair gleaming golden in the sun, her eyes as blue and bright as the nearby sea.

"Fair lady," said Fairhands, "this is not the welcome I had expected."

"And why not, Sir Knight, when you come armed from head to foot, sword at your side and spear in your hand? I want no more of murderous warriors here."

"How else should your true love and sworn

champion appear, but with the armor and weapons that saved you from your enemy?"

"I have heard that you are a great prince, and it was as such that I expected to see you. But if you are only a simple knight, then you can expect only my thanks. Earn great renown in twelve month's time, and we can then speak of love."

"Lyoness, from you I deserve greater thanks and less coldness. My deeds in your behalf were worthy. They were accomplished because of my willingness to shed my last drop of blood for your sake."

As the young knight finished speaking, the lady went from the window. Then the drawbridge came down. The portcullis was pulled up and a young page came forth.

"Follow me, Sir Knight."

Fairhands did so and presently found himself in a great hall hung with rich tapestries of courtly scenes. Minstrels were tuning their

instruments aloft in the gallery. Serving men were hurrying back and forth carrying table linens and plates of silver gilt and gold.

The page led Fairhands to one of two thronelike chairs at the high table and then departed.

Time passed slowly and Fairhands, alone   61

with his bitter thoughts, grew impatient.

He was on the point of leaving the hall and castle when Lyoness entered. Her dress was as blue as her eyes, her jewels as golden as her loose-flowing hair. In beauty she far outshone the princesses in the tapestries.

At the sight of Lyoness, Fairhands found his love flourishing once again.

She sat beside him and looked ardently into his face.

A great feast was served them, but Fairhands and his lady had thoughts only for each other.

At last Lyoness spoke.

"Fairhands, your bravery can be equaled by no one. Your noble birth has been proven by the manner in which you received my heartless taunts and cruel words. I am beholden to you more than to any man living."

The knight took her hands in his own. "Will you then pledge yourself to me?"

"With all my heart, for you are my first love and I could love no other."

"Then," said Fairhands, kneeling, "I promise to be loving and true throughout the length of my life."

And thus it was at Michaelmas time in King Arthur's castle by the sea that Sir Gareth, known as Fairhands, wed the Lady Lyoness before a great host of lords and ladies and knights of the Round Table.

64